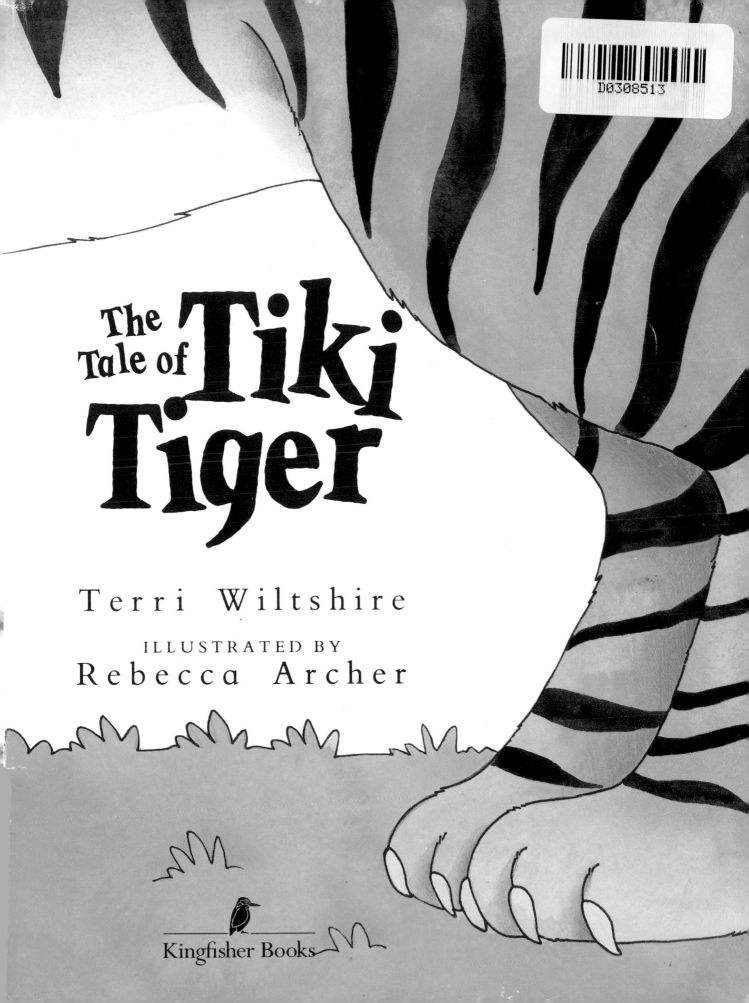

The Tale of Tiki Tiger

Terri Wiltshire

ILLUSTRATED BY
Rebecca Archer

Kingfisher Books

It was the day of
the Jungle Jamboree.
Tiki Tiger was very excited.
"I must look my best,"
said Tiki. "I'm doing
something extra-special
today."

The monkeys were swinging in the trees, practising for the climbing contest. Swish, swoosh, swish.

"Tiki," called the monkeys, "come and practise with us." "No thanks," said Tiki. "I'm doing something extra-special today."

The crocodiles waddled
down to the river to practise
for the swimming contest.
Galumph, galumph, galumph.

"Come and swim with us,
Tiki," said the crocodiles.
"No thanks," said Tiki.
"No time for swimming.
I'm doing something
extra-special today."

The lizards scampered
in front of Tiki.
They were training
for the Jamboree race.
Tippety, tippety, tippety.

"We'll give you a practice race, Tiki," cried the lizards. "Sorry, I have to go," said Tiki. "I'm doing something extra-special today."

The deer bounded by, rehearsing their leaps. Hop, skip, s-p-r-i-n-g.

"Are you in the leaping contest, too?" the deer asked Tiki.
"Not me," said Tiki.
"I'm doing something extra-special today."

Down by the river, all
the animals gathered together.
They clambered aboard boats
decorated with flowers
and vines and ribbons.

And in the boat in front, the grandest of all, was Tiki Tiger.
"I'm leading the parade," said Tiki. "Let the Jungle Jamboree begin!"

Kingfisher Books, Grisewood & Dempsey Ltd,
Elsley House, 24–30 Great Titchfield Street, London W1P 7AD

First published in 1993 by Kingfisher Books
2 4 6 8 10 9 7 5 3 1

BRITISH LIBRARY CATALOGUING IN PUBLICATION DATA
A catalogue record for this book is available from the British Library.

ISBN 1 85697 107 4

Printed in Hong Kong